Mystery on the Midway

The Dallas O'Neil Mysteries

MYSTERY ON THE MIDWAY

by

JERRY B. JENKINS

MOODY PRESS
CHICAGO

ISBN:0-8024-8385-2

2 3 4 5 6 Printing/LC/Year 93 92 91 90 89

Printed in the United States of America

To Daniel Jenkins,
childhood best friend

Contents

1

Acres of Fun

Whenever our family passes the huge amusement park on the expressway, my little sisters, Amy and Jennifer, and I beg our parents to take us. "I wanna ride the upside-down rolly coaster again!" Jennifer squeals.

She was way too small for a ride like that. I don't know where she got it in her head that she had ever ridden it. That roller coaster was monstrous and fast, and it turned you upside down four times in less than a minute. It had been only a couple of years since I had been tall enough to ride it.

Mom and Dad had taken us to Acres of Fun at least once a year for as long as I could remember. We would spend the whole day, going on all the rides, seeing a few of the musical shows, and staying away from the arcades and shows my parents thought weren't good for us.

It was easy to stay away from that stuff, because it was limited to the southeast corner of the park. If you didn't walk across the Arcade Bridge you never saw the part of the park designed for teenagers and adults. There was no age limit, but you hardly ever saw families heading that way.

Once last summer my dad sent me to the lost and found booth next to the Arcade Bridge to look for Amy's softball cap. She had left it in a bumper car.

A man took my name and phone number and said he would call if it turned up. "But don't count on it, son. People rarely turn in hats."

As I turned to leave, three kids who looked like they were in their late teens walked past. The one in the middle wore a green cap with a white bill, but I couldn't see the front to know if it said "G.S.L." for Girls Softball League. Without thinking, I followed the guys.

Before I knew it I was across the Arcade Bridge, and even though I lost sight of the teenagers and never saw them again, I was close enough to the arcades to hear the music. Besides the funny sounding calliope, much like the one in the family section of the park, there was also Dixieland and rock and blues. I was fascinated.

So this was what we were supposed to stay away from! I didn't want to get any closer to the midway, a broad walkway with tents on either side. From where I stood, my face burning with the guilt of not having scampered right back across the bridge as soon as I realized where I was, I got a taste of what was in those tents.

One was full of video games turned up so loud I could hear them from a hundred feet away. Another had a sign that said "Freak Show." I had heard there was a man with fins and scales like a fish. There was also supposed to be a live, two-headed cow. A man with a small, portable microphone stood on a platform before a long curtain, urging people to pay a dollar to see "The World's Largest Sea Monster." He said the beast was "tons of violence and death, but he's out of the water now." I admit it: I wished I'd had the time and the money.

At another tent a sign promised that a woman would turn into a gorilla. "One hundred thousand dollars to anyone who proves she's not alive!"

From a trailer behind one of the tents three beautiful women in scanty costumes slipped into the tent, and more music began. Some kind of a show, I guessed. All up and down the rest of the midway were games and challenges, weight and age guessers, ring tosses, shooting galleries, and what my mother always called gyp joints. "They just take money from people who don't know better," she'd say.

I looked at my watch. If I didn't meet my dad at a hotdog stand at one, he would come looking for me. I had three minutes. I ran.

"What took so long?" he asked.

"I thought I saw a guy with our cap," I said, panting. "I lost him though."

I said nothing about the Arcade Bridge or the midway, but I was strangely silent the rest of the day. I found myself thinking about nothing but what I had seen. It wasn't that I wanted to disobey or even to do anything wrong. I was just curious, wondering what I was missing. What could be wrong with seeing things other people see all the time?

Over the next several weeks I thought a lot more about Acres of Fun, and especially about the forbidden Arcade Bridge. Shouldn't I know about these things so I could understand what was wrong with them? How could I even be normal if I was sheltered from that whole side of life?

I knew that section of the park was seedy and loud. I didn't want to live like the people who worked there or went there. I was just curious. Was I tempted? I told myself I wasn't. I would have felt terribly guilty if I wasted my money or saw something I knew would be displeasing to God or my parents. But what if I just walked down the midway and looked around? I wouldn't go inside any of the tents. I wouldn't spend any money. I would just see what it was all about, and then my curiosity would be satisfied. I would never go back or even think about it again.

Not long after that I started bugging my parents to let me go to Acres of Fun with some of my friends from the Baker Street Sports Club. Mom and Dad fought it for a long time, but I could tell I was wearing them down when they quit saying no right away and did a lot of private talking.

They had been trying to give me more and more freedom lately, letting me make certain decisions and help them set some of my rules. They said it was because I had learned to do my work without complaining or having to be told several times. I had also quit pestering Amy and Jennifer and getting so angry when they bothered me.

Most of all, Mom and Dad said, they were pleased that I was reading my Bible everyday, memorizing verses, and telling my friends about Christ. Several of the kids in the Baker Street Sports Club had become Christians. They and some of the others wanted to go to Acres of Fun some day, and without any adults. We worked and worked on our parents, trying to convince them we were old enough, responsible enough, obedient enough.

After a few weeks my dad started quizzing me rather than shutting me off when I raised the idea. "How long would you boys be at the park?"

"We'd leave at sundown. Can we do it, Dad?"

"I'm not sure yet, Dal. Don't keep asking. What would you do for money?"

"We're saving up. Once you pay to get in, the only thing that costs is food and games."

"I don't want you wasting your money on video games and all that."

"I know, Dad. I won't."

"And you wouldn't be allowed over in the arcade area, that midway across the bridge.

"I know."

I had no intention of going over there, and I knew that if I was with the guys and they were watching me, I wouldn't have the guts to sneak. I might be curious and would see how close I

12

could get without actually walking through, but I didn't plan to disobey.

I could tell Dad was going to let me go. Lots of the other guys had already been to Acres of Fun by themselves, but this would be the first time I would be allowed. It would be great, especially with a bunch from the sports club.

Once I knew my dad was coming around, I started talking it up even more at our clubhouse, the new shed behind our old barn. I wanted to know how many could and would be going.

"I still can't believe you're going to get to go without your parents," Cory said, his red hair bouncing. "You never get to do anything."

I wanted to defend my parents, to say that they were being the best mom and dad they knew how, but I was so excited about maybe getting to go that I just nodded. They were pretty straight, but they were starting to loosen up. If I could prove myself on this one, maybe they'd give me a lot more privileges. They sure gave me a lot of responsibilities.

"Count me in," Cory said. "I've been there a million times. Anyway, my grandparents gave me a bunch of money for Christmas that I still haven't used."

"I'll go," Bugsy said. A wiry black kid, Bugsy smiled shyly. Everyone jerked around to look at him. He was nodding. "I know I said my mama would never let me," he said, "but she said if I was hangin' around with that wonderful O'Neil boy, she knew I wouldn't get into any trouble."

He had imitated his mother when he said, "That wonderful O'Neil boy," and everybody hooted and hollered.

Jack Bastable, a retarded boy who was the biggest kid in the club and one of the best athletes, raised his hand.

"Yes, Jack?"

"That's just about what my dad said. He said to ask you if you could watch me because my sisters can't come."

I looked down. We all loved Jack, but who wanted to be saddled with that responsibility all day?

"I'll be good," he insisted. "I'm no trouble, really."

"Yeah, well, we'll talk about it," I said.

My best friend, Jimmy Calabresi, spoke up. "We can trade off bein' in charge of Jack," he said. " 'Course he can go."

Jack beamed.

I wanted to tell Jimmy that was easy for him to say. He'd be the first one to forget it was his turn, and I'd wind up keeping track of Jack.

I liked Jack—don't get me wrong. But going to an amusement park for the day was one thing; baby-sitting was another. If Jack sensed my hesitation, he didn't show it. Jimmy had said in front of everyone that Jack could come, so he was coming.

"Have you got money?" I asked, a final chance to talk him out of it.

He nodded, grinning. "Dad said if you could handle me, it'd be worth it to him!"

Great.

I had one more idea. Kyle! The strawberry blond, the fast-talking sports expert had helped watch Jack before. I looked right at him. "You comin'?"

He shook his head. "No money."

"Take a couple of turns watching Jack, and I'll pay your way."

He smiled. "You got yourself a deal."

"OK, so it's Cory and Jimmy and Jack and Kyle and me. Who else?"

The rest had excuses, at least all but Nate. He sat there stocky, behind thick glasses under whitish blond hair. He had no excuse, but he didn't say anything either.

"How about it, Nate?" I said.

"Maybe, maybe not," he said. "If I come I'm not sure I want to hang around you guys all day."

My smile froze. "Well, excuse us."

Everybody laughed except Nate. "You gonna play leader, captain, coach, parent, and all that, just like you do around here?"

14

I didn't deserve that. I was elected captain and president by everybody, Nate included.

"I'm not planning on running anything," I said. "I'm just trying to get a group together so we can have some fun."

"Yeah, and I s'pose you're gonna tell our mommies if we do anything you wouldn't do."

I didn't know what to say. Why was Nate being like this? What had I ever done to him? "I'm only finding out who wants to go," I said. "You going or not?"

"None of your business," he said. "If you see me there, you'll know. If you don't, you won't."

2

Begging to Go

Nobody could figure out what was bothering Nate, even though we'd had trouble like that with him before. In fact, he wasn't the only one who'd had a bad attitude. Before Cory became a Christian, he'd been tough to deal with. He still had a temper, and there were times he'd mouth off and then have to apologize.

But with Nate it was different. None of us could forget the time our first clubhouse had burned. I had to ask the guys individually if they'd had anything to do with it. It turned out none of them had, but the way Nate acted made us suspect him until we learned the truth. He had been trying to keep from me that he and Kyle had been working on a trick football play, but still there had been no reason for him to act mean.

I didn't know why, but neither Nate nor Cory had ever been too happy having to answer to their friend—me—as leader of the Baker Street Sports Club. I would have given up the job in a minute if I'd thought that's what the rest of the guys wanted. But they didn't. They liked things just the way they were. I just wished they would have defended me against Nate. He made me feel awful, and I didn't feel like defending myself.

That night I finally put the question to my dad, flat out. "Dad, it seems you're close to deciding that I can go to Acres of Fun some day with my friends. What can I do to earn it?"

"Now there's an interesting approach," he said, smiling. "I don't want you to have to earn it. You've been doing pretty well with your jobs and with obeyin' and not terrorizin' your sisters. I can always count on you to get stuff done and to be fairly cheerful. I'm not as worried about how responsible you are as I am about what you're gonna do at Acres of Fun for a whole day. You know, even the price of the food out there is a crime."

"I know, Dad, but I don't want to be the only one bringing a sack lunch. I'll look like an idiot."

"Isn't there a picnic area there?"

"Yeah, but Dad—"

"See, Dal, that's what bothers me. For as mature as you are, you worry too much about what your friends think. Seems like your mother and I get calls from parents all the time here about what a nice boy you are and how you're a good model for their boys."

"Aw, Dad—"

"We're real proud of you for that, Dallas. Why don't you use some of that natural leadership you musta got from your mother and tell these friends of yours that they should save their money, pack lunches, and eat in the picnic area? You guys can buy your drinks at the park, though even that goes against my grain. You'll spend five times as much for a soft drink there as you would in the grocery store."

"But we can't take drinks into the park."

"I know. That's how they get your money. It's ridiculous."

"But, Dad, it's my money!"

"I know it's your money. Is that the way you want to spend it? Wastefully?"

I shrugged.

18

"You're comin' close to talkin' me out of lettin' you go, Dal."

"Why?"

He leaned forward and rested his elbows on his knees. "Because even though it's your money, I'm in charge of teachin' you how to use it wisely. And this isn't wise."

I decided not to argue any more. How could I? Even though it was my money and it seemed to me I ought to have the right to even waste it if I wanted, I couldn't tell him it was wise. He and Mom had hammered it into me that all my money, not just the part I put in the offering plate at church, belonged to God. That was why it had been wrong for me to pay a friend two dollars for a candy bar I could have gotten at the store for fifty cents.

I had been showing off, trying to convince everybody I had the money and that I really wanted the candy. It was one of those situations you get into where everybody is watching and listening, you say something stupid, and then you refuse to back down. Jimmy once paid nine dollars for the right to finish some kid's ice-cream cone. Later he told me, "Dal, it was the worst thing I ever ate. Am I stupid or what?"

What was I supposed to say to that?

Now I was just waiting and hoping. I knew if Dad let me go to Acres of Fun he would pile up a few rules for me. Maybe by waiting me out the way he had done, he was setting me up to agree to all of them—no matter how many or how embarrassing they might be. If that was his plan, it worked. I would have agreed to anything.

Later that night I started getting calls from the guys who were going. They were excited, and somehow they got the idea that I already had permission. I felt a little guilty about not telling them, but I was sure it was just a matter of time.

The next day Dad asked me to take a walk with him in the field. He wore his khakis and tee shirt and scuffed along in his construction boots. "Tell me who else is plannin' on goin'," he said.

"Jimmy, Bugsy, Cory—"

"The redhead?"

"Yeah."

"The one who's started comin' to our church?"

"Yeah. And Kyle."

"Kyle? Who's that?"

"He's the fast-talking guy who knows everything there is to know about sports but isn't that good at many of them. He was our kicker in football."

"Oh, yeah. Who else?"

"Nate and—"

"I don't know him, do I? Who is he?"

"Stocky, blond, thick glasses."

"Oh, uh-huh. Kind of a hothead, an attitude?"

"He's all right."

"Keep an eye on him. He could be trouble."

"Dad, I'm not in charge at the park. It's not like this is an official club outing or something."

"Is Jack goin'?"

"Yes, and Kyle will help — "

"If Jack's going, someone's gonna hafta watch him, Dallas. His sister going?"

"No, we're going to trade off. I wish we didn't have to."

"Yeah, but you want him to come, don't you?"

I shrugged. "Not really. He's going to be in the way."

Dad stopped walking and glared at me. "Dallas!"

"I don't mean anything by that, Dad. But it'd be a lot more fun if we didn't have to be bothered with him."

Dad ran his hand through his hair and sat on the ground. "Let me tell you something, Dal."

"I know, Dad. I shouldn't have said that. I was the one who got Jack into our club, and we all like him. He's a great athlete and a nice, innocent guy. But—"

20

"Listen to me. All of our lives would be easier and more fun if we didn't have to worry about anyone else. What kind of a life do you think your mom and I would have if we didn't have three kids?"

That stopped me. I'd never thought of that. "You can get baby-sitters," I said.

"You're still our responsibility, twenty-four hours a day."

I nodded.

"Frankly, the fact that Jack is goin' is the best thing I've heard about this deal."

Ouch! I had missed my chance. I should have told him how thrilled we were about Jack's going, how we were planning to trade off watching him, and all that. But I wouldn't lie to my dad. "What's so good about him going, Dad?"

"It'll make you more responsible. At least it should. I would hope you, at least, would be aware of where Jack is all the time, even if it isn't your turn to watch him."

"Yeah, I probably will. I wish I could say I was happy about it."

My dad sighed and shook his head. "I guess I shouldn't expect so much from you, Dal, but you're going to learn, sooner or later, that life is too short to live only for your own pleasure."

"Do you think that's what I'm doing, Dad?"

He ignored the question and kept talking. "Before you know it, you'll turn around and you'll be in your thirties, be married, have kids, and realize that it's more important what you do for others than what you get for yourself."

I was getting impatient. I wanted to interrupt and ask Dad if I could go or not, but I knew that would kill the idea. He would tell me in his own time. I mean, he had taken me out there for something.

"I'm going to let you go, Dal," he said. "And I hope I don't have to tell you what to do and what not to do."

"No, you don't," I said. "I know."

"I hope so."

"I do."

"I'm tempted to give you a whole list of rules and regulations, but I shouldn't have to."

"I know."

"You know the rules, don't you?"

I nodded.

"Where you can go and not go, what you can do and not do?"

I kept nodding.

"You guys ridin' your bikes?"

"Yup."

"They've got a place there for 'em, so you can lock 'em?"

"Right."

"You can be there when it opens, but I want you to leave at dark, like you said."

I agreed immediately, even though we all would have loved to have stayed until the park closed at nine-thirty. "But I can't speak for the other guys, Dad."

"Frankly, I don't care about them either. You know what I mean."

"Yeah."

"I mean, I care that they get home all right, but they're not my responsibility, and you are. Of course, you need to see to it that Jack gets home."

"That'll be the responsibility of whoever's watching him then."

"Make sure it's you."

"Dad—"

"I mean it. I don't care whose turn it is. You take the last shift with Jack and make sure he gets home OK. You know you're the most responsible kid in the group, and so does everybody else."

"Not everybody."

"Well, their parents know. That's my last rule: you've got Jack at dark, OK?"

"OK. Thanks, Dad."

The sun was setting, and the grass was dewy. Dad rose slowly and headed back to the house. I followed him, noticing how slow and tired he seemed. The last thing I ever wanted to do was anything he told me not to, anything that would disappoint him or cause him any trouble.

By the time I got to the house, however, I was thinking only about my phone calls. I had to call Jimmy, Cory, Bugsy, Kyle, Nate, and Jack.

We would be going to Acres of Fun the following Saturday for the whole day, with no parents.

3

Freedom

Probably because I had an idea what Nate's reaction would be, I saved his call till last. Everyone else was excited as we planned to meet at Toboggan Road and Baker Street at eight-thirty the next Saturday. It would take us about a half hour to ride to Acres of Fun, so we would be there when the gates opened.

Nate was difficult, as usual. "What're you saying?" he asked. "That I have to ride with you guys?"

"No, but—"

"I thought you said this wasn't an official Baker Street Sports Club deal."

"It's not, Nate. It's just that—"

"It's just that you want to be in charge and tell everybody what to do and tell who's gonna baby-sit the retard and—"

"Now wait a minute, Nate. We agreed we would never call anyone names, and we certainly aren't going to start calling Jack names. That's a pretty cruel thing to do to a kid as nice as—"

"Awright, O'Neil! Gimme a break! I still don't want to baby-sit, and I don't wanna ride with you guys or hang around with you guys or be bossed around by you."

"Nate, I don't know what your problem is, but I wasn't planning on bossing anybody around. You can come and not worry about me, and even though I think you should be a good friend and help out with Jack, I can't make you."

"You sure can't, but I'd like to see you try."

I sighed. I couldn't win. I didn't know what I had done or not done or what I should do or not do. He didn't seem in the mood to explain himself, so I just asked him if he was coming or not.

"What do you care? I'm not ridin' with you, and I'd only hang around with you guys if I felt like it, so maybe I will and maybe I won't. Fair enough?"

"Well, fair isn't what I'd call it, but I get the message."

"Good," he said. And he hung up.

Some guys you just can't figure. I was as surprised as anyone the next Saturday when I was not the first one at the corner for the bike caravan to Acres of Fun. Usually I'm the first to show up at those things because I feel I'm supposed to organize everything, even if it isn't a sports club activity.

So who should be there but Nate? He seemed cheerful enough, eyes sleepy behind his glasses, so I decided not to risk setting him off by saying, "Hey, I thought you weren't riding with us!" There wasn't much else to talk about, so I didn't say anything. I noticed Nate wasn't carrying a bag or a backpack, and I was grateful my dad hadn't followed through on his idea of making me bring my lunch. I knew it would be expensive to eat at the park, but I don't know if I could have handled the embarrassment of being the only one with a brown paper bag of sandwiches.

Jimmy was the next to arrive, chunky and dark-haired, pumping furiously until he discovered he wasn't late. Then came Kyle, talking a mile a minute about all the pro and college games he was missing on TV that day to be with us.

"We're so grateful," Nate said, and I could sense his mood changing.

Bugsy skidded up to us, his deep brown face alive with a smile and wide eyes. "Sorry I'm late! Let's go!"

"You're not late," I said. "We're still waiting for Jack and Cory."

"Oh, yeah."

Nate scowled and shook his head. "You guys can hang around waitin' for them. Not me! Anybody wanna get goin'?"

I can't tell you how disappointed I was when Kyle immediately volunteered. "I'm outta here," he said. "C'mon, Nate!"

They both raced off down the road without another word, but about a minute later, Kyle came charging back, squinting under his blond bangs. "Ah, almost forgot, O'Neil. I don't have enough money. I've got enough for eats and treats, but you were gonna pay my way in, remember?"

I studied him. "I remember," I said, "but there was a reason, wasn't there?"

"I know, I know. I'm s'posed to take a turn with Jack. No problem." He looked down the road. Nate hadn't waited for him. "C'mon, O'Neil," he said. "How 'bout it?"

I shouldn't have, but I stalled. "Well, don't you even want to know when your shift is?"

"Yeah, OK, when is it?"

I dug in my pocket for my list. The others gathered around to hear their assignments. "I have myself down for the first two hours (nine to eleven A.M.) and the last two hours (seven to nine P.M.). Jimmy will take eleven A.M. to one P.M., Cory one to three, Kyle three to five, and Bugsy five to seven."

"Oh, man!" Kyle said. "I don't want three to five! How 'bout lettin' me have the last one so I can have fun and not worry about Jack till the end?"

"Nah," I said. "I need to take the last one so I make sure I know where he is at dark and can get him home."

He pursed his lips and thought. "At least let me have the second to last shift, then, huh?"

"I don't care if you want to trade with somebody."

"Who's got the five to seven?" Kyle asked.

Bugsy said he did. "I'll trade," he said. "I don't care."

"Deal!" Kyle said. "Thanks, Bugs. Now lemme have the money, O'Neil."

I wasn't excited about giving it to him, even though I had planned to. I guess I expected him to be more grateful and more willing to earn it. I took my time getting the money from my wallet and counting it out. Kyle kept looking down the road. By now Nate was out of sight. All we could see was the Bastable station wagon in the distance.

Jimmy spoke up, surprising me. "You know, Dallas, none of us thinks it's fair that Kyle gets paid to do what we all volunteered to do."

I was stunned. I hadn't even thought of that. I stopped counting the money. "Hey!" Kyle shouted. "No going back on your promise!"

"I know," I said. "But Jimmy's right. I can't pay for everybody."

Kyle had his hand out and shifted from foot to foot, eager to get going. "C'mon, c'mon!" he said.

Jimmy spoke for the rest of the guys again. "It isn't that we want our way paid, Dallas. It's just that we think it's pretty rotten of Kyle to expect to get paid for doing something for our friend that we're all happy to do."

I felt guilty. Not only was I paying Kyle, like Jimmy said, but I knew I wasn't as willing as everyone else to help with Jack. Maybe that was why I had assigned myself two shifts. I knew down deep that I had done that only to make myself feel better and to avoid asking the others to take longer periods to make up for Nate's unwillingness to help.

I sighed impatiently and handed the money to Kyle. He stuffed the bills into his jeans pocket and sped off to catch Nate. The rest of us might have been tempted to grumble about his attitude if Mr. Bastable hadn't pulled up just then with Jack beside him, his bike in the back of the car.

Big Jack tumbled out and lumbered around to the back as if he couldn't wait for his dad to free his bike. He smiled and greeted everybody while I showed Mr. Bastable my schedule of who would watch Jack when. We chatted while Mr. Bastable removed Jack's bike from the car, and as Jack walked it over to join the others, Mr. Bastable pulled me aside.

"I want you to know how much Jack's mother and I appreciate this, Dallas. We really do." He pulled some cash from his pocket. "Here is Jack's money to get in, some more for food, some extra for incidentals, and I want to pay your way in, too."

"Oh, that's not necessary, Mr. Bastable, really."

"No, I insist," he said. "I'm also giving you an extra ten dollars so you can give a couple to each of the guys who takes a turn, but I'd appreciate Jack not knowing about that."

"You really don't have to do this," I said.

"I know, but we want to, so let us."

He pushed the bills into my hand, and I thanked him. "Would you care if I also split up the money you gave me and gave some to each of the guys?"

"That's up to you, Dallas. Can I count on you to ride home with Jack?"

"Right. We'll leave the park when the sky is dark, so we should be to your place a half hour or forty-five minutes later."

"Good. I know you know this, but remember that Jack, even though he's six-four and over two hundred pounds, is gentle and is a child emotionally. He's a wonderful, sweet kid, but he can also be stubborn and childish at times, so you have to treat him the way you treat your little sisters. You may have to tell him no and insist that he does something he doesn't want to do or doesn't do something he wants to do. If you have to, you may tell him to do what you say or you'll tell me. That usually gets his attention."

I nodded.

"Thanks again, Dallas." Mr. Bastable moved to Jack, and they hugged each other. "You behave and do what your friends say, OK?"

Jack nodded. "You bet!" he said. "Friends! Acres of Fun!"

We got to the park a few minutes after nine and could hardly believe the crowds. Hundreds were ahead of us by the time we rode between the parked cars and parked and locked our bikes. Nate and Kyle were nowhere in sight, probably already well inside the park.

"I'll see you at one by the Ferris wheel," Cory announced, curled strands of red hair poking out beneath his baseball cap. "And I'll keep track of Jack till three, right?"

"OK," I said. "Where you goin'?"

"I'm going with Bugsy. We're gonna see how many rides we can get on before one."

"You don't wanna have lunch with us?"

"Nah. See you at one."

Bugsy and Cory ran to get into another line.

Jimmy stood there looking forlorn. Jack turned around and around, looking at everything: the people behind us and in front of us, the people in the lines on either side, the cars pulling in by the hundreds, the ornate gates through which everyone would pass, the gigantic rides in the distance.

"How about you hang with Jack and me during my shift, Jimmy, and I'll stay with you for your shift? We can do everything we want and have lunch before we meet Cory at one."

Jimmy shrugged. "I guess so. Either that or I'm on my own."

"Well, you want to go with us, don't you?"

He shrugged again. "Why not?"

That wasn't the reaction I had hoped for, but I know he felt the same way I did when everyone else seemed to run off on their own. I knew this wasn't a sports club deal, but did everyone have to make it so obvious that they were thrilled about not having to answer to anyone, especially me? What had I done to turn everyone off? Or were they just enjoying their freedom?

As we moved closer to the ticket booths and the people in front of us turned to glare at big Jack, who was crowding them in his excitement, I knew I wouldn't really enjoy myself until Jimmy and I were on our own.

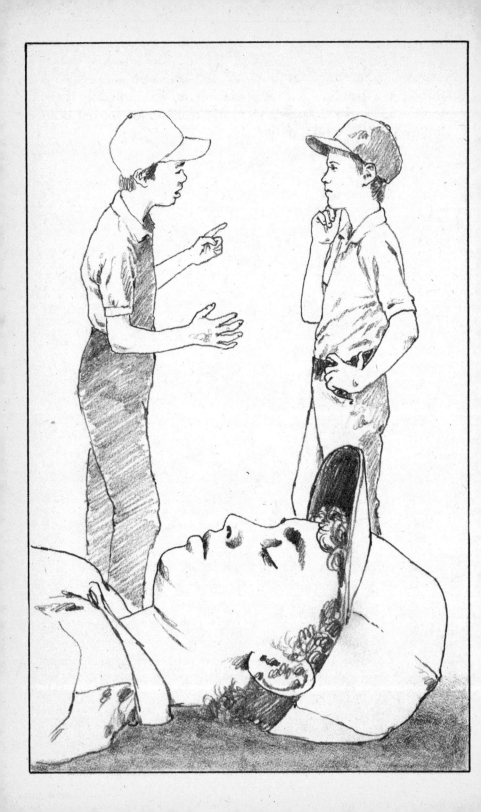

4

Feeling the Heat

Keeping track of Jack and seeing that he got on all the rides he wanted was more fun than taking a small kid. When I had to take my little sisters around, I was bored to death watching them ride in tiny, stationary cars. Jack loved the rides the way a kid would, but he was big enough for the adult attractions. And he was fearless.

We took him on the Giant Squid, and he laughed till he cried. The Space Dive turned us upside down four times, and Jimmy made me ride next to Jack. That wasn't so bad, but when we got on the Perpetual Motion Centrifugal Force Shaker, I sat on the outside, Jimmy in the middle, and Jack on the inside. As soon as that colossal thing started whirling, Jack was thrown into Jimmy and Jimmy into me. My sides were splitting. I thought that ride would never end.

Just as Mr. Bastable said, we had to keep Jack in line. He wanted me to buy everything for him, from cheap trinkets to teddy bears. And he wanted popcorn, cotton candy, pop, hotdogs, you name it. I kept telling him no. "We'll be having lunch at noon." But he kept begging.

As the sun rose higher, the temperature rose. I finally broke down and bought us each a cheap hat. Cheap but not inexpensive. I thought immediately of my dad and what he might think of my paying three times for a hat what I would pay in a store.

Even under the hats, we were soaked with sweat. The lines to and from the water rides were hundreds of people long. But it was almost worth the wait. We put Jack ahead of us in the log ride, and he laughed heartily when he was doused. He insisted on getting back in line, but I couldn't let him. We would have waited almost an hour to ride again. Within minutes the sun had dried us.

Jimmy and I didn't make a big deal of it at eleven when it became his turn to be responsible for Jack. I felt a little freer and less tense, but still I had to make Jack obey. Jimmy wasn't tough enough and would have given in if I hadn't stood up for him.

Finally, it was lunch time. We decided to buy our stuff at the concession stand nearest the Ferris wheel, so that we could rest and take our time and still be there when Cory showed up for his shift with Jack. We hadn't planned well. The lines at the food stands were long, and the lines at the rides grew shorter.

Jack wanted four hot dogs, three bags of chips, and two large Cokes. I talked him into two, one, and one, promising that if he was still hungry, we'd get more. We moved to a picnic table in the shade and fought the flies for our food. Jimmy prayed.

We finished eating by twelve-thirty, and I enjoyed the chance to sit and do nothing for a while. Carefree as a child, big Jack stretched out on the ground and soon fell asleep.

Jimmy had an idea. "Hey, Dal, I know it's my turn to watch Jack, but the line for the Space Dive is the shortest it's been all day. Let me go over there, and I'll take your last shift with Jack."

"What? You're gonna trade two hours for a half hour?"

"Yeah! How 'bout it, Dal?"

"Wait a minute! I'll be with you the whole time anyway! What's the difference?"

"No! I'll watch Jack myself. You'll be free."

"Big deal, Jim! Who wants to be alone at Acres of Fun? That's no fun."

"Suit yourself."

"Well, maybe it'd be all right. I'd have to find you guys about a half hour before dark, though, because I promised to take the last shift, and I hafta take Jack home."

"Good, then you won't feel so guilty. You'll only be trading me an hour and a half for a half hour."

"Go!"

Jimmy dropped his trash in a basket and charged off to the Space Dive. I suddenly felt very drowsy, but I didn't dare fall asleep in that muggy, humid spot. I was afraid I would sleep right through it if Jack woke up and wandered off. When Cory showed up, about ten after one, I was surprised that Jimmy was not back yet.

"Where's Bugsy?" I asked.

"He's off on his own," Cory said. "He didn't want to bother with Jack until it was his turn."

"That's what he said?"

"Not exactly, but that's what he meant. I don't blame him. I mean, I'm willing and all that, but I'd rather not, if you know what I mean."

"I know."

"Did you and Jimmy watch him together?"

"Yeah. Worked out OK."

"I'm not too excited about the big guy bein' asleep."

"Hey," I said. "This has been the easiest part."

"Maybe, but I want to get movin'. Bugsy and I spent the morning across the Arcade Bridge, and I'm ready for some rides."

"You guys were in the arcades?"

"Yeah. Great shows. Great fun."

I shook my head. It seemed like none of my business, but Cory was a Christian. I thought about lecturing him about what he allowed into his mind through his eyes and ears and about the ways he spent his money. But hadn't I just spent an incredible amount on lunch, not to mention the caps? And didn't I really wish I could sneak a peek at what was happening across the bridge?

I left it alone. Cory woke Jack, and they headed off to the rides. Maybe it's something you get out of your system, I thought. Surely Cory wouldn't take Jack to the arcades. Or would he? I ran after them but lost them in the crowd. I prayed Cory would have more sense than that. What would I tell Jack's parents?

I headed back to the table where we'd had lunch. Jimmy was waiting for me, looking pale and tired. "What'sa matter, Jim?"

"Sick! I threw up on the Space Dive."

I almost laughed out loud. "Really? What happened?"

"Remind me never to go on that thing right after lunch! The people waiting in line weren't too thrilled with me!"

"You all right now?"

"Not really. I think I'd better lie down awhile. You can go on alone."

"No, I'll stay with you. It's no fun alone."

"Dallas, I feel worse knowing that I'm holding you up. Go ahead and find something to do. Try me in an hour or so."

"All right. I'll be back here at two."

Wandering around that enormous park for the next forty-five minutes, I didn't see one person I knew. I looked for Bugsy for a while, wondering if he wanted anyone to hang around with. No sight of him. I strolled through all the rides and family shows, finally ending up near the remote control cars and boats. I drove a couple of them, but with no one to share the fun, I didn't find it fun at all.

Without having planned it, I wound up on a bench under a canopy on a walkway that led to the Arcade Bridge. When I realized where I was I didn't even turn to look. I just listened. There was that noisy calliope again.

36

My mind flashed back to my first look at the arcades across the bridge. That stuff sure sounded fun and exciting and interesting. What could be wrong with seeing that sea monster? Or the lady who turned into a gorilla. I mean, I knew that couldn't be real, but what about that prize if anybody could prove it wasn't? And a two-headed cow? Now there was something that had to be seen to be believed. The picture on the canvas outside that tent showed a black and white cow with two heads, both bowed and eating grass. I wanted to see that.

But I knew better. There was a lot more offered down that midway, and even though I had a lot of money in my pockets, it wasn't intended to be wasted on that junk. In spite of myself though, I turned and looked over my shoulder, past the crowds and across the bridge to the rows and rows of tents and booths.

I looked older than I was. Maybe I could fool one of the age guessers and win a prize. I also looked lighter than I weighed. What if I could win a teddy bear for each of my sisters? But then what would I say about how I had gotten them?

I looked at my watch. Time to get back to Jimmy. I hoped he felt better. I was getting bored and didn't want to be tempted any more. The arcades sure wouldn't be boring, but they would be wrong. I would be disobeying, spending my money unwisely, and would feel guilty. Knowing me, I would have to confess to my parents right away or I wouldn't be able to sleep.

On my way back to where I had left Jimmy, I noticed very little. I wasn't aware of people, wasn't looking for anyone in particular, and knew all the rides without studying them. There was no doubt about it: this side of the park had very little exciting to offer compared to what was on the other side of the Arcade Bridge.

Jimmy was still at the picnic table when I arrived. "How ya doin', pardner?" I asked.

"Not so good," he said.

"You gonna be sick again?"

"No, but I sure don't feel like doing anything for a while. I'll be OK in another hour or so. Did you find any of the other guys?"

"No, but maybe I'll try," I said. "You gonna be all right here?"

"Sure. Thanks, Dal. You probably ought to be here when Cory brings Jack back at three anyway, huh? To make sure Kyle gets together with them?"

"It's not Kyle at three, remember? Kyle traded with Bugsy. Maybe I'll try to find Bugsy to make sure he remembers."

"Good idea."

I had just lied. I had no intention of looking for Bugsy. Who would know the difference if I didn't look for him but did what I really wanted to do? I could come back and say I hadn't seen him anywhere. I had a better chance of not seeing him than seeing him in that big park anyway. If I did happen to stumble onto him, so much the better.

But I was heading for the Arcade Bridge. I pushed from my mind every negative thought, every twinge of guilt, every reminder of who I was and Whose I was, every instruction from my father. I started walking. My heart raced, my eyes seemed to be able to see only straight ahead. I would not go into any booths, I promised myself. I was just looking, just checking it out. Anyway, it was broad daylight. What if someone I knew saw me going in or out of any of the attractions?

This way, if someone wondered what I was doing wandering around that end of the park, I could tell them I was looking for a friend. For the briefest second I was stunned at how quickly I had started rationalizing lying, even to myself. One thing I really believed, however, and that was that I was only going to look. I should have known better. I should have asked myself what would be the fun in that. I should have wondered how I would get a closer look and still decide not to get involved, but I didn't. I told myself what I was doing was normal and innocent and explainable.

Arcade Bridge, here I come!

5

A Closer Look

I was determined to only look. Really, I was. I believed that if I just boldly strode across that bridge and walked past every attraction in the arcades without going in, I would satisfy my curiosity.

Had my father really said I couldn't even walk by them? The first time we talked about it he had made it clear he didn't want me over there. But surely he wouldn't mind if I just walked past. The second time we talked about it he reminded me that I knew where he wanted me to go and not go. That wasn't very specific. I hadn't actually promised. Had I?

Just across the bridge was the calliope. That was innocent enough. It reminded me of the children's circus programs I'd watched on television when I was real little. An old man worked the complicated controls, getting the unique sound out of it. He made it puff steam, clang bells, whack cymbals, and play that airy organ sound. I was the only person watching. Everyone else passed him as if he were in the wrong end of the park. Which he probably was.

Farther down was a Dixieland band. Nothing wrong with that, I decided. My mother enjoys some of that kind of music, often saying she's impressed with the brass and woodwinds and the lively beat.

Several couples danced on the hot asphalt in front of the bandstand, which was something I'd never seen my parents do. Mom once told me she wouldn't have much problem with dancing either if everyone stayed with his own spouse. "There's certainly nothing wrong with embracing the person you love and moving to good music," she'd say, "but it doesn't seem like something you'd want to do in public, and certainly not where someone else's husband or wife wants to cut in. Anyway, wherever I've seen public dancing, smoking and drinking are never far away."

My dad told me that the reason he didn't want me going to school and community dances was that he thought they would make it difficult to keep from becoming tempted. "There's plenty of time for you become attracted to girls," he'd say, "without having to worry about impure thoughts. God gave you eyes and a mind, and even gave you a natural attraction for the opposite sex so you can enjoy your wife someday. But why make staying pure difficult for yourself by putting yourself in a place where women are dancing around in front of you? Nobody dances only with the one they love, so everybody gets a little casual about who they act friendly with."

I had to admit he was right. I'd seen dances at school after basketball games or ones held in the other side of the gym during fun fairs. Watching girls dance was great fun, and imagining myself feeling free to dance with one or several, like a lot of guys were doing, almost made me light-headed.

What I liked about the way my dad talked about it was that he didn't make it sound wrong to be attracted to girls and to look forward to holding and loving your wife someday.

"Physical love is a beautiful gift from God," he'd say. "It's not to be spoiled by getting mixed up with lust or by becoming too involved with someone before you're married."

That's why I felt guilty watching the young couples dancing and changing partners to the Dixieland music. I didn't leave as quickly as I should have, and when I was gone I wished I could go back. But I didn't. I moved to the video arcade where dozens of games were blaring. I had played video games before, but I had never seen so many in one place, and I couldn't believe the noise.

From the outside I peered over the shoulders of kids playing games I recognized, and I wished I could try them and see how my scores compared with theirs. I had lots of money in my pockets, but I was just looking, after all. Almost all the kids in the arcade looked older than I was. A lot of them were smoking. Some even carried cups of beer, which were not allowed on the other side of the Arcade Bridge. One thing that didn't interest me or tempt me was the T-shirts most of these kids were wearing. They had skulls and crossbones, daggers, and blood. Maybe those kids thought that was cool or rebellious or independent or something, or maybe I was too young to want to think about or even look at such violent and scary stuff.

Still, I wouldn't have minded trying a few of the games, in spite of the noise from the machines and the music videos thundering from screens up in the corners. I had my hand on the bills in my pocket when I talked myself into moving on.

A rock band with a name I'd never heard was playing at a small pavilion up the midway, and a couple of hundred people moved and clapped with the music. I stood at the back, near one of the loudspeakers, and watched. I've never liked rock the way a lot of my friends do, but the beat made me want to move. The lead guitarist played so well you had to admire the practice he must have put into it.

Still, I didn't understand why the band had to dress and look so sloppy. It would have been all right for them to look a little different or in a way that made it clear they were performers, but for some reason they looked as if they wanted to dress as bad as possible. That made me feel alone. I realized I was a very straight, very boring, very normal kid, and that it showed. I was definitely not cool.

The only bands on the family side of the park had been another, bigger, Dixieland group and a country and western band. They looked very country and dressed different than I ever would, but I thought they looked nice. The men wore country shirts and jeans with cowboy hats and boots. The women wore frilly, colorful dresses and boots. People square danced to their lively music, which looked like fun but made me wonder what my mother would think of all that partner changing.

Just before I got to the freak-show tents, I passed one other music act. The sign said simply "Blues." The musicians played the piano, an electric bass guitar, and a clarinet. It was different music, just instrumental, and the players were obviously good. They dressed in what looked like old fashioned suits with skinny ties and sunglasses, and a lot of their audience looked the same. The clarinetist also played trumpet on some songs, and the melody seemed to have a mind of its own.

I enjoyed a lot of it, but the songs didn't seem to have a direction or a satisfying end. The musicians would play together, and then one would take a solo, adding his own personality to the melody. It was almost as if they tried to top each other. I liked that a lot, but I was beginning to run short of time.

I hurried to the tent that advertised a live fishman. Painted on a big sign was a man who appeared to have a green, scaly body, sort of like how mermaids are supposed to look. His head looked normal, but his arms and legs had scales. His feet were not shown, but from what the rest of him looked like, I wondered if they were webbed or stuck together like a fishtail.

A recording played over and over: "Trapped in a body that belongs in the deep, the Fishman's gills became lungs that allow him to make the best of life in the open air. He thinks and talks and acts like a man, but he has the body of a large fish. He's half man, half fish. He's the Fishman! Come in and meet him. Talk to him. The Fishman."

I had never been so curious in my life. And I couldn't understand the reactions of the people who went in and came out a few minutes later.

"Why did you ask him that?" a girl asked her boyfriend.

"They said we could talk to him and ask him questions," he said.

"Yeah, but you talked to him like he was dumb or something!"

"Well, it was like talkin' to an animal. How did I know he could understand?"

"He spoke English!"

"Yeah. Where do you suppose he learned that? He musta been born underwater."

Another couple came out laughing, the man saying over and over, "I told you! I told you! Didn't I tell you?"

And the woman said, "Yes, yes! You told me. Don't rub it in. I'm still glad I checked it out."

The strangest reaction came from a teen-age girl who came out with three friends. She was crying. "That was so sad," she said. "So cruel. How could they treat anybody that way?"

Her friends laughed it off. "I'll bet he gets paid good money," one said.

"Where would he spend it?" the crying girl asked. "Would you want to appear in public looking like that?"

"What're you talkin' about? He's used to it! He appears in public all the time! That's how he makes his living!"

"Yeah, but on the street, in a store, where people don't know he's a professional . . . "

I wanted to plunk down my dollars and get in there as fast as I could. I would have been willing to confess it to my parents and tell them that my curiosity got the best of me. It was all I could do to keep moving. I wanted to see that Fishman so bad I could feel it throughout my whole body.

In the next tent was the two-headed cow. Many of the people coming out of there had the same reactions as the ones who had seen the Fishman. Only now they were feeling sorry for a cow and how it was being used to make money. Some said, "Don't waste your money!" to those of us hanging around outside. That only made me want to see it more. Why was it a waste of money? The painting made the cow look huge, and it would be interesting, yeah, a learning experience, to see a cow with such a birth defect. Wouldn't it?

All around me were guys trying to talk girls into going in with them. Everyone laughed when one girl was trying to talk her boyfriend into seeing the cow, and he didn't want to. She finally dragged him in. A few minutes later she came out alone, shaking her head, disgusted. He followed a minute later, laughing. "Sure glad we didn't miss that!"

That should have been a clue for me, but still I wished I could take a peek. I tried to see around the corner, but the tent booth was designed to allow those of us on the outside to hear a little of what was going on inside but not to be able to see anything without paying a few dollars.

The World's Largest Sea Monster was next. I wondered if this creature was related to the Fishman. "He's out of the water now," the man kept saying. And this creature wasn't hidden in a booth. People paid their money and walked up six steps to where they could look at the monster over a drape-covered railing. I watched several step up, look at it, look at each other, shake their heads, and keep looking at it as they moved slowly along the platform to the other end. Then they came down the same number of steps on the other side, but they didn't talk the way the others had, coming from the previous shows.

Some seemed to study the creature longer than others. Some even stopped and leaned over, peering carefully at it, as if studying it. Surely, this was an animal I should take a closer look at. I could learn something from this. As I watched I noticed what looked like a huge fin appear above the rail and then turn back down again, out of sight. Had it been my imagination?

No, a few minutes later, there it was again. The platform was more than thirty feet long, but it couldn't be very deep or wide. Was that gigantic sea beast turning and rolling in a compact chamber of water? I was so curious, and the exhibit looked so interesting, that I decided I might tell my parents about it and ask them to take me to see it sometime. They might not want to spend that much time in the arcade area, but an exhibit like that might persuade them.

I moved past the next tent, a larger one with brassy music coming from it. The sign said "Burlesque Show, Under 16 Not Admitted." For some reason, knowing I couldn't get in there if I wanted to made it easier for me to not think so much about it.

I was curious. I was tempted. But there was no legal way to get in anyway, and I certainly wasn't going to sneak in. Frankly, I knew there was no way I could ever justify that, or even justify seeing such a show if they did let twelve-year-olds in.

I looked at my watch. It was after three. I didn't panic. I assumed Bugsy would remember the trade of shifts with Kyle and would take Jack until five. Though I wouldn't be there to make sure the switch was made, Jimmy was there. He could handle it. I would definitely be there at five to make sure Kyle was still willing to take his shift.

And just like that I had given myself almost two hours to do what I wanted. The question was, What did I really want to do? I decided to eventually head back and find Jimmy. I wouldn't be bringing him to the arcades or even telling him I was there, but on the route back to the bridge were several other smaller booths. Now that I could take my time, I would at least find out what they were about.

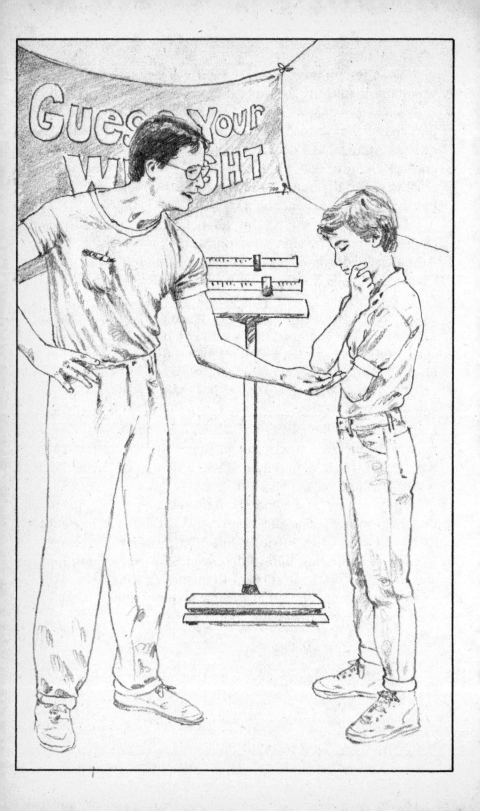

6

The Lure

I stood at the back of the crowd at the weight and age guessing booth. I expected the guesser to be an old expert, but in truth he looked like a high schooler or a young collegian. He was slight and wore glasses, but his voice sounded assured over the loudspeaker.

"If I can't come within two years, you win the grand prize. Your choice. C'mon now, you know you don't look your age. People been tellin' you all your life they can't believe you're that old, or that young—or that alive!"

I didn't think that was that funny, but it drew a huge laugh. Friends and family pushed each other into letting the guesser try. He came up to a man with gray hair and a white beard who stood with two boys, one about my age, the other younger.

"Are you going to try it, Grandpa?" one boy said.

"Try it, Grandpa," the other added.

"Oh, I don't know " the man said. "I s'pose it would be harder for him to guess someone of my vintage than it would be for him to guess one of you."

"That's right, pop," the guesser teased. "Take a chance —win a teddy bear. Take it home to Grandma."

The man looked knowingly at the boys. "All righty. How much?"

The guesser took his money and asked him to take off his sunglasses. He studied the man, looking him up and down. He then wrote a figure on a sheet of paper and asked the man how old he was."

"Thirty-eight! Want me to prove it?"

"No need. I believe it. I guessed forty."

The man shook his head, and the kids smiled with embarrassment. "He's not really our grandpa," they announced. "He's our dad!"

The guesser shrugged as if that was no news to him. "It's time for my break, folks! Come back in a few minutes, and win yourself a teddy bear."

The guesser put down the microphone and leaned against the side rail of his booth. While he pulled a cigarette from a pack in his shirt pocket, I approached him.

"How did you do that?" I asked. "I would have guessed that guy in his fifties."

At first I wondered if he would think I'd been rude. There was no reason for him to give away his secrets or tricks or whatever it was that allowed him to be right often enough to make money. I even wondered if he had someone planted in the audience who won occasionally, or someone else who drifted around and got a good idea how old someone was and tipped him off.

But he didn't hesitate. It was as if he had been hoping someone would ask. "It's easy, kid," he said, blowing smoke over my head. "A lot easier than it looks. First, those kids called him Grandpa, and they said it pretty naturally. You'd be surprised how many people try to pull that stunt, but they say it so loud and obviously it's like they think they're in some play. Or like they think I'm a total fool. So, I discount right away what somebody calls somebody else. My clues come from the person himself.

"That guy I just guessed was wearin' docksider shoes with no socks, cutoff jeans, a half-sleeve shirt that buttoned, and even though his hair was gray, it was cut and styled like a middle-ager, not an old-timer. Grandpas don't wear those clothes or style their hair that way. But the dead giveaway, in fact what made me think I might have guessed too old even, was when I had him take off his sunglasses.

"The eyes were bright and clear, not bloodshot and tired from age. No wrinkles or bags under the eyes, no crow's feet at the corners."

"Crow's feet?"

"Those tiny little wrinkles at the corners when an older man smiles. This guy was smooth as glass. He's nobody's grandfather."

I nodded. "Pretty good."

"I impressed the twelve-year-old, did I?" he said.

I nearly jumped. "How did you know that?"

"I guessed," he said, smiling.

"Really, how did you do that? Were you sure?"

"Not totally. I toyed with saying thirteen. I would have still been close, right?"

"At the end of the summer I'll be thirteen."

He smiled and nodded.

"What did I do to give that away?"

"Kids are easy, pal. They really are. I mean you're here alone, so you're over ten. Your clothes are a little young for a teenager, at least one who's been a teenager a while. But the softness is still in your face, and you aren't too cool to ask questions. Fourteen, fifteen, that'll be beneath you."

"Wow."

"Impressed?"

"Yeah."

"You wanna be a guesser someday?"

"Nope. No way."

"Good for you. You don't seem like the kind of a guy who would want to make his living ripping people off."

"Ripping people off? You didn't cheat anybody."

"Sure I did. I cheat everybody. The only person I haven't cheated today is you. I keep more of the money than I'm supposed to. If I can find a way, I stash some of the prizes too. Any way to make an extra buck."

"You lie to your boss then? Is that what you're saying?"

"Exactly. You don't lie, do you?"

My stomach went cold. I had lied already that day. "I try not to," I said.

"Good for you."

"But what did you mean about ripping off everybody? What if somebody beats you. People do beat you, don't they?"

He shook his head with a small smile. "Nobody."

"C'mon! You guess everybody's age within two years?!"

"Nope. More than half the people who challenge me walk away with a big, beautiful teddy bear."

"See?"

"No, son, you don't see. Look here." He held out three dollar bills in his palm. "This is what a person gives me to guess his age. OK?"

I nodded.

"I guess wrong, I keep the money and give him his prize. Right?"

I nodded again.

He folded the bills and jammed them in his pocket.

"But what if you're wrong? Then the guy wins."

"What does he win?"

"He wins that teddy bear."

"But who has the three dollars?"

"You do, but he has the prize."

"Big question still out there, boy. How much did that bear cost me?"

I shrugged. "I don't know," I said. "How much?"

He smiled a yellow-toothed grin, reached deep into his other pants pocket, and pulled his hand out in a fist. He turned

52

his hand over, almost under my chin, and slowly opened his fingers to expose the coin on his palm.

It was a quarter.

"Know what I do with the weights? I make sure I guess low. Flatters 'em. If they're real big, I tell 'em they don't even have to prove it to me. I'll believe 'em. What do I care? I clear two-seventy-five even when I lose. Only difference to me is a quarter, so why embarrass 'em? Stay out of the arcades, kid."

He grabbed the microphone. "OK! Who'll be next? Bet I can guess your weight within three pounds! Who'd believe how much, or how little, you weigh? Just three bucks, and look what you win!"

I don't know why, but when I walked away from the young guesser my legs felt weak. It was as if I had learned a huge, painless lesson, and I had been shown some strange kindness by a man who had little going for him. He was not like anyone I had ever spoken with before. He was not honest, not hardworking. He took advantage of people, ripped them off, as he said. And yet he had been nice to me, had seemed almost to care for me because of my innocent questions. I'm sure that because I was impressed with his ability and wanted to hear about it, he took an interest in me. I hardly knew what to think about it.

I knew the rest of the gyp joints were rip-offs, but I was still curious. At one booth people leaned over the counter with a stack of rubber rings in their hands and tried to toss them onto the necks of old-fashioned pop bottles. It looked simple. Some people just flung them and let them flip in the air. Others tried to keep them as flat as possible. I stood there at least ten minutes and didn't see anyone make a ring land on a bottle.

Just as I was about to leave, a young couple came by with a crying baby in a stroller. The man had long hair and a beard and wore a black T-shirt with the short sleeves rolled up to his shoulders. He tried a couple of stacks of rings and then laughed while his wife tossed her stack all at once.

They bounced and skipped over all the bottles but didn't land where she wanted, and they both threw their heads back and laughed when they noticed the last ring in her stack had caught on her little finger and still hung there. The man picked up the baby, and when it wouldn't quiet down, he handed it to her. The baby immediately grew quiet, grabbed the ring from her hand, and studied it.

"Throw it, Bubba!" the woman squealed. "Can you throw it, honey?"

The baby put the ring in its mouth and gnawed on it. "Oh, icky! Baby! Bubba! No!" The woman yanked it from the baby's mouth and flung it into the bottles. The baby cried, the man looked embarrassed, and the woman began screaming. "We won! We won! Bubba! You did it. Oh, what do we get?"

A bored young woman with an apron full of rings and change came over and spoke softly. "I'm sorry, ma'am, but you're not allowed to put any foreign substances on the rings."

"What do you mean, foreign substances?"

"No glue, no spit. The baby had the ring in its mouth. That's why it landed on the bottle."

The woman swore and put the baby back in the stroller, where he continued to scream.

The man leaned across the counter. "Little lady," he said, quietly but fiercely, "if you don't want any trouble, you go pick out some cheap toy over there for our baby. It don't hafta be no big bear or nothin'. You jes' find somethin', or there ain't gonna be no more ring tossin' tonight."

"But, sir—"

The man put both hands on the edge of the counter and began to lift. When the woman saw the entire booth begin to shake, she ran to the prize pile and grabbed a small, furry ball and tossed it to the man.

Someone pressed past me and excused himself, but I ignored him to see how the angry man would react.

"Thanks," he said and gave the ball to the child.

My heart banged so loud I wondered if anyone else could hear it.

I walked past a rifle shooting gallery. People all up and down the line were firing and swearing, firing and swearing. There didn't seem to be any connection between how expert they looked with the weapon and how many things they hit. Those who won anything won plastic trinkets and mugs worth pennies. The big teddy bears and other prizes stayed put. I had no interest in trying my luck.

"A dollar for twenty nickels!" an old man shouted.

What kind of a deal was that? I wondered. I stepped closer. For a dollar you got a stack of nickels worth the same. If you got one of the nickels to land on a plate or saucer and stay there, you won a prize. People were buying nickels all over the place.

Almost everyone tossed them the same way, flat and carefully. I saw no one succeed all the time I stood there, but there were nickels on several plates and saucers. Had those been placed there, or had earlier tossers won?

I studied the nickels on the plates. They never moved. Not even when newly tossed nickels seemed to hit them. Were they glued on? I watched a young man toss his entire stack, one by one, at the same plate. Three times he seemed to succeed, only to see the nickel slip off the back.

"That thing's vibratin'!" he said, softly at first, then louder. "It's vibratin'! Ain't no way no nickel's gonna stay on there."

The man behind the counter hurried over. "We have a winner," he said, smiling. "That's your nickel right there, ain't it?"

He pointed to a coin that had been on a plate since I'd been there. The tosser hadn't even aimed at that plate. "We shore 'nough got us a winner, if that's y'all's nickel."

The young man smiled.

I didn't know if he was just happy to think he was cheating the game or if he knew he was part of a plan to cheat everyone else.

"That's mine, all right," he said. And as he took his teddy bear and walked away, he said it again. "All right!"

I looked at my watch to see how late it was. But my watch was gone.

7

Hook, Line, and Sinker

I couldn't imagine where I had lost my watch. I hadn't taken it off to wash my hands or anything like that. I had looked at it shortly after three. How late could it be? The sun was still fairly high in the sky. I didn't want to ask anyone what time it was, and I didn't want to be obvious about looking at someone's watch. I didn't see any clocks around. Where could I look at someone's watch without his knowing it? The shooting gallery!

Those people were so intense, concentrating on their targets, that they wouldn't even notice if I peeked at their watches. I hurried back and was reminded again why I had no interest in that crazy game. Shoot and swear, shoot and swear. That's all they did.

A short, stocky man in a serviceman's uniform slapped his money on the counter and was handed a rifle. He leaned both elbows on the counter and gently held the weapon to his eye. After he fired the second time and swore the second time, I sidled up next to him and glanced at his watch. It was after five!

I had spent more than two hours just watching what was going on on the midway. How could that much time have gotten away from me? And how could I ever figure out how I had lost my watch?

"You gave me a gun with a crooked barrel!" the serviceman shouted.

"Shut up!" someone else hollered.

"This gun's got a bent barrel, man!" the serviceman repeated.

A tall, thin man with wiry muscles approached him from behind. "Don't be givin' this booth man no trouble, soldier. He's my uncle. Anyway, you oughta know a rifle's a rifle and a gun's a gun. Whatcha doin' callin' a rifle a gun when you're in the army and oughta know better?"

The one in uniform put the rifle down and stepped close to the taller man. "You want to make something of it, son? I happen to be in the navy, not the army, and I'll call a weapon anything I want."

"Oh, yeah?" the tall man said, shoving him. "Maybe my uncle here and me would like to make somethin' of it."

And then I noticed. This was the same thin man who had caused the trouble at the ring toss booth, the one with the wife and baby! But where were they? Despite the potential violence right next to me, I looked past the men, looking for the woman and the baby. I didn't see them, but all up and down the counter men looked up from their shooting.

Necks craned, elbows still on the counter, they were riveted by the impending fight. The wiry man's uncle quickly came out from behind the counter and edged past the leaning men. "Excuse me, excuse me," he said, brushing past them.

"I'll bust you!" the wiry man shouted, and the crowd drew closer. But as he moved in to break up the fight, I saw his uncle drop three wallets into his own apron.

"It's all right, Spike," the older man said. "Leave him alone. I'm shuttin' down the booth for a while. Everybody out."

The guys at the counter, their attention distracted from the fight and their wallets, began complaining.

"I'm sorry, fellas," the counter man said. "Them's the rules. Any disturbance, we shut down for a while. Here, I'll give everybody fifty cents back."

That seemed to cool them down, and it also kept their hands in their front pockets and not where their wallets had been. The thing that really puzzled me was how quickly the two fighters lost interest in each other and went their separate ways.

I could hardly believe what I had seen. That was a setup! All three of those guys were in it together, just to steal wallets! And that tall guy must have worked some sort of a scam at every booth, once with a "wife" and a "baby" and again with an "uncle." While he causes a disturbance, someone else is pick-pocketing wallets. And stealing watches. I had seen magicians take watches right off people's wrists without their knowing it, but I didn't know thieves did it too.

I must have lost my watch at the ring toss booth when I was so scared watching the thin man threaten the counter girl. Someone had brushed by me during that commotion, but I didn't even look at him. How would I explain that one to my parents?

All I wanted to do now was get out of there fast. I knew I should tell somebody what I had seen, but what if one of those guys found out about it? Who knew what they might do to me? I ran down the midway and across the Arcade Bridge, into the crowds on the other side, hoping Jimmy would still be at the picnic table. Of course that would mean he was still sick, and I didn't want that. But if he wasn't there, how would I ever find him?

And he wasn't there.

Now what? How would I find out whether Kyle had taken Jack? All I could do was wait by the Ferris wheel until seven, when it would be my turn—well, Jimmy's and my turn. Should I run around trying to find someone, or should I go to the information booth and ask to have someone paged? I figured if there was a problem, they would have had me paged.

Everything must be all right. But then I might not have heard the page, if I didn't even notice when someone took my watch. That made me think to quickly check for my wallet. It was there. I switched it to my front pocket.

I talked myself into believing that everything had worked according to schedule. Bugsy had taken his turn, Kyle had taken his, and all I had to do was to be back at seven to take over.

I counted my money. I had a lot because of what Mr. Bastable had given me. I planned to split it up among the guys who watched Jack, but I hadn't promised anybody. I mean, he had given it to me for organizing everything. He would want me to have it. Also, that was money I didn't have to account for at home. No one knew I had it.

I headed straight back to the Arcade Bridge.

I had no interest in the calliope, the Dixieland band, the rock band, the blues band, or people dancing. I started at the Video Arcade where I used my only two quarters to play the game at the back edge of the tent. It was almost as if I wasn't really inside. I couldn't see the music videos, and no one stood in line at my game. If I took two steps backward, no one would have known I'd even been playing.

The first game ended before I had scored many points. I tried again, this time missing an extra play by less than fifty points. I took a dollar to the change machine. My next three games were mediocre, but the last one was a personal record for me. I placed 87th out of the top 100 who had played that day. Not bad for a kid who hadn't played the game except on Jimmy's TV. This time I changed a five dollar bill.

By the time I had spent twenty more quarters on the game and had finished only as high as 81st, I was bored with it, wondering what else was available. The driving machines looked fun. One had a screen that made it look and feel as if you were really on a race track. Curves, straightaways, barriers, crashes, oil slicks, the whole bit. It looked easy.

I watched another guy score tens of thousands of points before he quit. I didn't expect to do that well, but I didn't expect to not even make it around one lap of the track in my first two games. At the start the car behind me smashed into me. By the time I got restarted, I hit a sign at the side of the road. When I restarted again and pulled back onto the track, I hit another car. By the time the clock had run out, my heart was racing, but my car wasn't. "Novice" flashed on the screen.

Oh yeah? Watch this!

In the next game I made it around one and a quarter times and earned a beginner's rating. I needed another dollar changed. I don't know how much later I went through another five dollars' worth of quarters, learning and improving and almost mastering that road racing game. I didn't make the top 100 racers for that day, but I improved my score by more than 10,000 points.

I wanted to try every other game in there at least once, but now that I had talked myself into the arcades, there was much more I wanted to see and do. I headed out to the freak shows but passed my original game on the way. I changed one more dollar and played it four more times, not once approaching my best previous game.

All that did was ruin the satisfaction I had gotten from mastering the road racing game. I felt empty and a little guilty, deciding to put off till later what I was going to do about all this. I had almost perfected a video game, and what did I have to show for it?

I headed straight for the Fishman exhibit, but when I got there, I hesitated. I could rationalize playing video games (maybe not spending that much money, but what was wrong with a little fun?). It was something I'd done at friends' houses a lot. But could I explain seeing the Fishman? Was it educational enough?

A huge crowd, much bigger than before, teemed around the entrance where the recording bellowed over and over. I got in line. About twenty minutes later I joined a couple dozen others as we moved out of the sun and heat into the cool and dark of a tent I never dreamed I would enter.

Sitting in a folding chair behind a plain wood table was a man who looked like he was in his late thirties or early forties. His black hair was thinning in front, and his wide face looked friendly but sad. He wore old-fashioned, horn-rimmed glasses and seemed to look either far away or simply down at his hands, which were folded in front of him. At first I thought he was the announcer.

He wore a drab green muscle T-shirt, but he wasn't very muscular. Beneath the table I could see he was wearing dark pants, white socks, and thick-soled black shoes.

"Is everyone in?" he asked, looking up but not directly at anyone. "Can everyone see?"

A few people nodded, but one man called out, "See what?"

The man at the table, still sitting, separated from us by a bare metal rail, ignored the question and spoke softly. With his first words, several people jerked in surprise and stepped closer, me included. "I am the Fishman," he said. "I may have been born underwater, the offspring of a fish and a human. You may look but not touch, and you may ask any questions you want, but I will answer only those questions I choose."

This was the Fishman? I stepped closer and squinted. He sat under a single, unshaded light bulb, his hands still folded. Just below his chin he seemed to have a rash on his neck, pink near the top and then redder as it moved toward his shoulders, chest, and upper arms.

On his biceps were fiery red blotches. Starting just above his elbows and covering his elbows and forearms and the back of his hands were raised bumps that looked like extra growths of skin. It reminded me of my mother's uncle who had a problem with calcium deposits and had similar growths on his elbows.

This was a poor man with calcium deposits! His growths, or whatever they were, were red and yellow and white, not

64

even close to green or scaly. We all, I'm sure, felt as sorry for him as we felt ripped off. No one asked a single question. He looked embarrassed and even sadder than when we first saw him, and we filed out.

What a lesson! But still I wondered what the two-headed cow looked like. I had come this far. I was going to find out.

8

Snared

By now I was sick. Something told me I was going to check out everything I could on the arcade side of the bridge and that I was going to feel even worse about it later. Why did I do it? Why didn't I stop? What made me continue even when I knew I would regret it? What kind of a Christian was I anyway?

The people at the two-headed cow exhibit were letting in 30 people at a time, and I was in a line of more than 100. I watched and listened as people came out, and it was the same as before. Some laughed, some were sad, others looked blank.

When my group finally got in we found a dimly lit area covered with straw and smelling like cow barns usually smell. One cow rested in a corner in the dark. When we were all assembled, a man with a cattle prod in his hand stepped behind the rail and moved toward the animal. As soon as the cow saw it, she awkwardly rose and paced slowly toward the crowd. We leaned forward and squinted in the darkness. When the cow turned to one side and ambled past us, I saw it.

Her face seemed to have a smaller, misshapen second face growing out of one side.

"That's fake," someone grumbled.

"No, it isn't," someone else said. "If it was fake it would be more convincing. It's just a mutation. This is a poor, old cow that should have been twins. Twins that never developed."

The face that seemed to be growing out of the left side of its head looked like a mouth, part of a nose, and two closed eyes. There was nothing alive about it. It was just a growth and was so far from the painting on the front of the tent that I knew I had been ripped off again. Surprise, surprise.

When I left the tent I was one of those who wasn't smiling. I wasn't as angry about being gypped as I was about how they treated that pitiful cow. She was sure afraid of that prod, and she knew just what to do. She simply paraded herself past the gawking crowd every few minutes, then went back to the corner for a rest. She was no two-headed cow. Just a cow with a birth defect.

If that didn't cure of me of my curiosity about the freak shows, nothing would have. And it didn't. I still wanted to see the sea monster.

On my way, though, I saw a sign I hadn't noticed before. It showed a humungous pair of jeans, and an arrow pointed down an alleyway to a tent where people could see The World's Largest Man.

I headed down there, having lost all sense of doing what I knew was right. Outside the tent was no crowd. Maybe it had just opened or others had missed the sign too. Or maybe the tent was too far from the midway to draw people. I stood looking. There seemed to be no charge for admission, no one begging people to come in, nothing. The pants hanging above the entrance had to be a gag. No way one person would fill out those things.

I moved slowly toward the entrance and saw light inside. Someone was humming. I heard pages turning. I peeked around the edge of the canvas.

There, sitting in an enormous, blocky wood chair was the biggest man I had ever seen. He wore ankle-high black boots with thick soles and no socks. His legs were bare and seemed to be about two feet thick from the ankle to the thigh. He was humming. A magazine was in one hand and a can of bug spray in the other. His great belly extended out over his waist and seemed to hang between his legs. He held his magazine on it as if it were a desk, turning pages with one hand.

His triple chin rested on his protruding chest, and his little mouth and eyes looked out of place. He wore glasses on his giant nose. Every once in a while he would leave the magazine on his stomach, hide his glasses in his fleshy hand, shut his eyes tight, and spray the bug stuff in his long, black hair, around his head, down his back, and on his legs. He never quit humming.

He startled me when he suddenly looked at me, smiled, and said, "A customer! Come in, son!"

I looked behind me.

"You!" he said, still smiling. "C'mon in!"

He set his magazine on a stand beside him. It was *Popular Mechanics.* "Tipton Bearford's the name. Tip ton, get it? Ha, ha! Six hundred and seventy-three pounds, eighty-three inches around the old biscuit basket. Calves twice the size of the normal fat man's waist. Takes twenty thousand calories a day just to keep me alive, but what a life, huh?" At the end of his spiel he asked if I had any questions.

Boy, did I have questions! I shrugged and shook my head.

"Don't be afraid of me, boy! What's your name?"

"Dallas O'Neil, sir."

"Dallas!? Your name's as bad as mine. I sound like I was named after some lawyer. You were named after a city! You got a brother named Fort Worth?"

I shook my head.

"Are you married, Dallas? No, 'course you're not. Probably divorced. Well, at least I found out you could smile. What're you afraid of, boy? I could never catch you!"

I timidly, and too quietly, asked a question.

"I didn't hear that, Dallas."

"I said I wondered if you were happy."

"Oops! You're not playin' along with the program, son. I'm s'pose to be the jolly fat man who makes people feel good. I'm s'posed to satisfy your curiosity and make you not feel guilty for takin' advantage of the poor freaks and mutants of society. Now you wanna know if I'm happy."

"I'm sorry."

"Oh, it's all right. 'Course I'm not happy. Have you seen the Fishman?"

I nodded, ashamed.

"I'm happier'n he is, I'll tell you that. How 'bout the Sea Monster?"

I should have just said no, but I admitted, "That's next."

"Even I haven't seen that. Can't get up steps, you know."

"Oh."

"That's why I'm not happy. Can hardly walk. They push me around in a customized wheelchair. I don't even fit in the seat on the train. My wheelchair is attached in the aisle so I don't get rocked around too much. But as you can imagine, the heart is going, the joints are bad, and the blood pressure is off the charts."

I was sorry I had asked. But I was still curious. "How do you get a job like this?"

"Believe it or not, I answered an ad in a newspaper. Oh, hey!" He looked past me. "More customers! Come right on in, and check out the biggest man in captivity! Tipton Bearford's the name. Tip ton, get it? Ha, ha! Six hundred and seventy-three pounds, eighty-three inches around the old biscuit basket. Calves—"

I backed out, sorry I had gone in. I went straight to the Sea Monster, where the barker kept insisting, "He's out of the water now!"

I paid and moved slowly up the steps behind the rest of the crowd. Behind the curtain, more than thirty feet long, was a plastic fish with signs stuck in it, telling interesting facts about it. I couldn't believe it. He was out of the water now, all right!

I didn't read one of the signs. I just angrily pushed past everyone else and went down the steps at the other end. Not only had I disobeyed and done a lot of stupid things, but it hadn't even been worth it! I didn't even want to stop and figure how much money I had spent.

I jogged toward the bridge, suddenly braver than I had been all day. When I saw a young couple walking toward me I asked the man for the time. "About ten after seven," he said.

Oh, brother! I sprinted across the bridge toward the Ferris wheel.

A very worried, very cross, Jimmy waited for me. "Where have you been, O'Neil?"

"Why? What happened?"

"What do you mean what happened? What happened to you? I thought you were organizing this thing. Cory comes back from his one to three shift, and there's no Bugsy. Cory doesn't want to take a double shift, so he pawns Jack off on me. I figure you'll be back or Bugsy will show up, so I wait around for a while, then go looking for Bugsy. I find him, he tells me he forgot about the switch, he takes Jack, and then I can't find you.

"So now I'm on my own till five, and guess who doesn't show up? Kyle! And of course Bugsy didn't want any part of the five to seven shift, so I got stuck with that."

"I'm sorry, Jim—"

"Oh, sure you are."

"Listen, where's Jack now?

"He's with Kyle."

"Kyle? How'd Kyle get back into it?"

"He showed up about five-thirty actin' real sorry about stiffin' us and said he would take Jack for two hours."

"So he should be back any time."

"Yeah, he should be back by seven-thirty."

"What time is it now?"

"We've got about ten minutes. Where's your watch?"

"I don't know. I lost it."

Jimmy went to the picnic table and plopped down. "I'm still not feeling all that well."

"Sorry."

"You oughta be sorry. I expected the other guys to act like idiots, but not you. Where were you anyway?"

"I got hung up."

"I couldn't find you anywhere."

"Why didn't you have me paged?"

"I did! Three times! They said you must not be in the park because that page can be heard anywhere this side of the Arcade Bridge. I told 'em I knew you were here. You didn't leave the park, did you?"

I shook my head.

"Then why didn't you hear the page? They said you can hear it on the rides, in the washrooms, in the restaurants, everywhere."

"I dunno."

"The woman said if you were in the park you musta been on the other side of the bridge, but I told her there was no way."

I didn't say anything, but if we hadn't been in the shade, Jimmy would have been able to see my red face. I felt like a criminal.

"You never even thought you heard your name once?"

I shook my head.

"Where were you, man?"

"None of your business, OK?"

"Dallas! We're best friends!"

"Not if you don't quit bugging me!"

"Just tell me you never once heard a page that sounded like your name."

"I didn't."

He stared at me until I looked at him and then looked away.

"O'Neil," he said quietly. I stole another glance at him and looked away again. "You dog. You were across the Arcade Bridge, weren't you?"

I never wanted to lie so badly in my life. But I couldn't. I couldn't do that. I misled him earlier, and I had made him think the wrong thing when I didn't answer some other questions directly. But to lie to a direct question—I just couldn't do that.

"What difference does it make, Jimmy? I'm here now."

"You were! You were across the bridge! Cool!"

I wanted to tell him it wasn't cool, but that would be admitting that that's where I was, and I was hoping he'd drop the subject. But now he'd never let it go.

"I thought you'd never go to a place like that, Dallas! What were you doing over there? Did you see any freaks, win any prizes?"

I wanted to tell him I'd only lost a lot of money and a watch. But he kept pumping me.

"I didn't think your parents would let you do that. But what they don't know won't hurt them, right? Didn't your dad make staying on this side a rule, otherwise you couldn't go?"

He had, but I didn't nod or say anything.

"Dallas," Jimmy said, "this is too good to be true. I was sort of afraid when I started going to your church and then became a Christian that I wouldn't be able to do stuff like that. There's still time. You can trust Kyle. Take me over there. Show me what's good."

I could trust Kyle? That was a joke. That was the same kind of crazy thinking I had gotten into when I wanted to do what I wanted to do and didn't care whether it was right or not. And now I had done the worst thing ever. I had set a bad example for a new Christian. My best friend. If I could do it, why couldn't he do it?

"Jimmy," I said slowly, "we need to find Kyle and Jack. And then you and I need to talk."

"Great. We can talk when we're at the arcades. How much money do you have?"

"We're not talking at the arcades, Jim. As for money—" I reached behind me for my wallet. It was gone.

9

The Confession

I felt terrible. I was getting just what I deserved.

Jimmy said, "You look like you need to talk."

Boy, did I!

"First I need to be alone for a few minutes, Jim. Do you mind?"

"Nah. Whatever. You want me to leave or what?"

"If you're still feeling sick, you can stay here. I'll be back. If Kyle shows up with Jack, make sure Jack stays here until I can take over watching him, OK?"

Jimmy nodded, and I took off, looking for a place to be alone. That would be a trick. Where was I going to find a spot to be by myself among thousands of people? Yet I had to look. My heart was racing, my stomach sour. I had disobeyed my parents, disobeyed God, done a lot of things I knew weren't right, and I had to decide whether I felt bad because I had done them or because I had been caught. I decided it was both.

About halfway between the Space Dive and the Giant Squid was a row of concession and souvenir stands. Between them and the washrooms was about twenty feet of shrubbery. I ducked behind it and found myself alone. No one could see me, and I couldn't see anybody, but I could hear the crowds milling around.

I just plain felt guilty. I tried to pray, but it was hard. I found myself trying to still justify in my mind that I had not done anything all that terrible. I hadn't cheated anyone, hadn't stolen anything. I had avoided the burlesque show. But my conscience kept hammering away at me.

I knew it was God, reminding me that I had disobeyed. It wasn't my job to decide what was right and wrong. I had people in authority over me, my parents, and I knew what I was supposed to do and not do. And after everything I had seen, how much money I had wasted, and how cheated I had felt, I was finding out just what was wrong with the sleazy side of the park.

Finally I was able to pray. I knew this wasn't the time to simply praise God for who He was or to ask Him to bless my family and the missionaries. It was time to be specific about what I had done, how and why I knew it was wrong, and to trust the Bible verse that says that if we confess our sins, God is faithful to forgive them and to make us clean again. I prayed silently, but I prayed as honestly as I ever had, and I meant it like never before.

When I was finished confessing, I asked God what He wanted me to do. I knew He wouldn't actually speak out loud to me. He never had. But He sure had a way of speaking to me through my conscience. One of the first things I realized was how stupid and selfish and ignorant I had been. I was even reminded that the reason I hadn't found my wallet in my back pocket was that I had switched it to my front pocket to protect it from pickpockets. As I sat there praying, I felt for it. It was there.

Besides knowing that I would have to tell my parents, I also felt God wanted me to tell Jimmy all about it. Then I would have to divide up the rest of my money among the guys who helped watch Jack. And if there wasn't much left, which I was afraid of, I would have to add some of my own money from home.

When I finished praying I pulled out my wallet. Even with all the money I had brought and the money Mr. Bastable had given me, I had less than ten dollars left! Another thing I was going to have to do at the proper time was ask the Christians in the Baker Street Sports Club to pray for me. Their parents thought I was this great role model for my friends, but after today I knew better.

I still dreaded telling Jimmy and my parents, and I hated the idea of having spent so much money so foolishly. I had sure learned an expensive lesson. For some reason, even after I had confessed it all to God and asked for His forgiveness— even though I believed His promise—I still felt guilty. I guess that's because I was. I mean, I knew Jesus paid for my sin, so the real guilt was gone. But still I felt bad about it because I wished I hadn't done it and I wished no one had to know about it. But they did.

I headed back to find Jimmy, and—I hoped—Jack.

Only Jimmy was there.

"No Kyle or Jack?" I said.

"Not yet. Should we start lookin' for them?"

"In a while," I said. "I've got to talk to you first."

Twenty minutes later Jimmy looked as glum as I did. "I should feel guilty too," he said.

"Why?"

"Because I would have been just as eager to do what you did. In fact, I still envy you."

"Don't. Believe me, it's not worth it. I should have known it wouldn't be. I did know it wouldn't be."

"I still think you're a good guy, Dal."

"Thanks, but I'm not. I proved that to myself today."

"You made a mistake, but you admitted it. Give yourself a break."

"I don't want to give myself a break. I hate myself for this."

"And you think you have to tell your parents?"

I nodded.

"That'll be tough. They think the sun rises and sets on you."

"Not really. They know me better than anyone else does. This won't be a total shock."

"It'll be total disappointment, though."

"Oh, thanks, Jim. That helped."

"Sorry."

"It's all right. It's true. It's gonna hurt them and me."

Jimmy looked at his watch. "It's eight o'clock, Dal. We'd better page Kyle."

"Let's look for him first. I'm sure they don't want kids paging each other all the time."

"Yeah, but if they knew Jack was retarded, they'd let us."

"I know, but let's try to find them on our own first."

We looked everywhere. The odd thing is that we never saw anyone else we knew either. That always surprises me. How can there be so many people at an amusement park close to where we live, yet we hardly ever run into neighbors, church people, kids from school, or even the kids we came with?

At eight-thirty I asked Jim to stay by the Ferris wheel just in case, and I went to the information booth and asked them to page Kyle and Jack. They weren't too happy about it, but I told them Jack was retarded and that it was my turn to take over watching him. The message announced over the loudspeakers asked either or both of the boys to meet Jimmy or Dallas at the Ferris wheel as soon as possible.

"If they're in the park, on this side of the Arcade Bridge, no matter where they are or what they're doing, they can hear the page," the woman told me.

That turned out to be bad news. After Jimmy and I had waited another fifteen minutes, we could only assume the worst. Kyle had taken Jack across the bridge. They were at the arcades.

We ran.

For the first time that day I saw someone I knew. As we headed across the Arcade Bridge, Bugsy came running the other way.

"Boy, am I glad I ran into you," he said. "We were all in the video arcade, and I ran out of money. Can I get a loan?"

I shook my head. "I'm not gonna lend you any money for the arcades," I said. "They're not worth it."

"How would you know? I wanna see the Fishman and the two-headed cow!"

"Trust me. Now who was at the video place?"

"All the guys."

"Everybody? Even Kyle and Jack?"

"Hm—lemme see. Cory and Nate and, yeah, Kyle and Jack. I think."

"You think? Don't you know?"

"Well, you know how video games are. You forget how long you've been playing, who's there and not there, who's already left, all that."

"You think Jack and Kyle maybe already left there?"

"I dunno. Listen, you're really not gonna lend me any money?"

"No."

"How 'bout you, Jimmy?"

"Sorry, Bugs. I'm broke."

"Then tell the other guys I'll meet 'em at the bike rack at dark. I'm goin' on some of the free rides till then. See ya!"

He ran off, and we hurried to the video arcade.

Cory was the only one there. He was irritated that we bugged him during his game. To our question about where everyone was, he jerked his head toward the midway. "The rock band, I think," he said.

"Oh, great," I said. "I can't wait till Jack tells his father where we took him."

None of the guys were anywhere near the rock band, so we split up and checked the other two music shows. I found nothing. Jimmy had run into Nate.

"Boy, is he in a mood," Jimmy said. "He told me to mind my own business and that no, he would not be meeting us at the bike racks at dark. He was staying till the park closed, and if we didn't like it we knew what we could do about it. I asked him if he'd seen any of the other guys, and he said he wouldn't tell me if he had."

"We're on our own again," I said. "It's just you and me looking for Kyle and Jack. Everyone else is accounted for."

I couldn't get out of my mind what a mess this would be if we had to call Mr. Bastable or my dad and tell them we had lost track of Jack. And what if something really did happen to him? I wondered if I could ever forgive myself. I knew the Bible said my sins would find me out and that there's always a price to pay. I just hoped it wasn't a high one that included one of my best friends.

"You wanna split up again?" Jimmy suggested.

"No. I just want to find them before the sun goes down."

10

Frantic Search

As the sun slowly dropped past the colossal rides in the distance, Jimmy and I sprinted through the arcades, looking for Kyle and Jack. We scanned the crowd at the Fishman exhibit, and when we didn't see them, I asked a man coming out if he had seen a tall, dark-haired kid and a strawberry blond boy in there.

"If they was in there, they'd be comin' out, wouldn't they?"

I shrugged. That was true enough, but you never knew with Kyle. I began to turn away when the man's girl friend spoke up. "I saw some kids like that at the fat man tent," she said. "Was there something wrong with the big one?"

"Like what?" I said, not because I didn't know but because I wanted to know if she meant he appeared retarded or if something else had happened to him today that would wind up being my fault.

"Like he's slow or retarded or something?"

"That's him," I said. "Thanks."

The fat man remembered me, and he also remembered Kyle and Jack. "The little one wasn't too patient with the big one, I'm sorry to tell ya."

"What do you mean?" I asked.

"He kept hurryin' him along. Told him there was lots more to do, more money to spend."

I shook my head. "Wonderful. I don't suppose you know where they're headed."

"Nope. Lots of great stuff to see around here, though, right?" The fat man looked sad again.

We kept searching. No one had seen Kyle or Jack at the Sea Monster either. That left the gyp joints, the last place I wanted to go. I wondered if I would see that same con man, the one who had caused a disturbance at the ring toss and the shooting gallery. What if he recognized me? What if he would steal my wallet? Maybe something like that was happening to Kyle and Jack right now.

Jimmy and I were running again.

"Hey!" Jimmy said. "What's this? Did you go to this?"

I looked at the sign. How had I missed that? It was the booth with the woman who turned into a gorilla. That was one I had wanted to see, but in my speed and my confusion—while doing so much that I knew I wasn't supposed to—I had missed it the second time around.

"Maybe they're in here," Jimmy said. "I hope they're in here. I'd like to see this, you know, just out of curiosity. Nobody told me I couldn't be on this side of the park. Want me to go in there and check for you?"

"I thought you were broke, Jim," I said.

"Yeah, but you're not. Are you?"

"Almost."

"Make up your minds, boys," the barker said. "One more minute and nobody gets in there. No one admitted after the show starts."

"I can't, Jimmy," I said. "I still feel guilty from last time."

"Yeah, but what if they're in there?"

"I just can't."

"Then I will. Fork over some dough!"

84

I fished a few bills out of my pocket. Jimmy grabbed them, slid them under the window to the man, and hurried behind the curtain. I paced. What if they weren't in there and we were just wasting time? Maybe I should keep looking, but I sure didn't want to go to the gyp joints by myself.

I approached the window as the man was pulling down the shade, indicating that no one else would be allowed in. "Listen," I said, "you don't happen to remember two guys comin' in here—"

"Are you kiddin'?" he said. "Lots of guys went in here. What'd they look like?"

"One was about my age, blond hair. He was with a big, tall kid who looked older."

"Oh, yeah, a dummy?"

"Well—"

"I mean a slow kid? A retarded kid?"

"Yeah!"

"They're in there now."

"Really? I gotta go in!"

"I just shut the cash drawer."

"I'll pay, and you can put it in later."

"Nah, go ahead. Just hurry."

I slipped in behind the curtain, just as the lights were going down. I couldn't see anything in the darkness. I didn't know where Jack and Kyle might be. I couldn't even see Jimmy. They were probably among the first in, and I knew Jimmy had to be somewhere close by.

There were no seats. When a spotlight shone on a curtain draped across a long wire, I saw the silhouettes of maybe a hundred heads. Way over in the corner one towered above the rest. That had to be Jack. But we were pressed in there shoulder to shoulder. No way I could get to him. I only hoped he would have to get out the same way we had gone in. I could wait for him at the door. I was glad to just know where he was.

The light shone on what looked like an old circus wagon with a jail door padlocked shut on the back. As the dim light inside the trailer came up, we could see a girl standing back from the door. She wore a swimming suit and stood perfectly still with her eyes closed. I wondered if she was really there or was only reflected in a mirror. I also wondered if she was real or just a painting, but she looked real. Then I could see that she was breathing. Her eyelids fluttered occasionally too.

Every few seconds the image of her was blurred, and she seemed to be growing hair. Someone off stage was telling a myth about some ancient creature that changed forms, and finally the images switched back and forth and back and forth until the girl was gone and a gorilla, or someone in a gorilla suit, stood in her place. A guard by the door of the trailer stood ready with a shotgun.

A few people snickered. Others laughed. Some gasped when the creature moved from deep in the trailer to the locked door, beat on its chest, and made gorilla noises. The guard pointed the gun at the beast. A few women in the crowd squealed. Suddenly the gorilla charged the door and beat on it, grabbing it and shaking it, trying to pull it off its hinges.

Then the door broke free! The guard was shooting. Everyone, men and women, screamed and yelled and surged toward me to get out. The lights went out, and we were left with the image of the gorilla escaping and coming toward us, the guard shooting at it.

As soon as we were out into the air again, people laughed. They realized the whole thing had been staged. It was all part of the show. The girl was a reflection, the gorilla was someone in a costume, the door wasn't really locked, the guard was shooting blanks. Everyone had paid for a cheap thrill, and they dispersed in the night. No one could prove the girl or the person in the gorilla suit wasn't alive, so the reward money was safe.

Jimmy landed next to me, pale but laughing his head off.

"Watch for Jack and Kyle," I said.

We did, but either they didn't show or we missed them. I tried to look inside the tent, but a guard stopped me. "Next show in fifteen minutes," he said.

"Did everybody get out?" I asked. "A couple of my friends are still in there, I think."

"Everybody got out," he said. "A couple of guys slipped under the canvas on the far side. We tell 'em not to, but it happens all the time, especially to the people farthest from the entrance. They're gone."

Jimmy and I went around to the other side of the tent. From there Kyle and Jack could have gone anywhere. The walkway straight ahead went right to the gyp joints. We had no choice. We had to find them. It was getting dark now.

I scanned the crowd at the ring toss and the nickel toss. Nothing. But there! At the shooting gallery! There was the thin man.

"That's the guy I told you about, Jim! C'mon! Let's see what he tries this time!"

We hurried over. I kept an eye on the man. He stood near the back of the crowd and seemed to watch without much interest.

"Watch this," I said to Jimmy. "That girl shooting, second from the left, is the same one who was with him at the ring toss earlier. I wonder if he'll stick up for his 'uncle' and pick a fight with her."

He didn't. She started the commotion. "Hey, this rifle's no good! It's not shooting! Hey! Honey!"

She turned and looked pleadingly at the tall man. As he strode forward, swearing and demanding to see the counter man, she slipped behind the row of other shooters. While the man grabbed the counter man's shirt, just under his collar, and pulled him forward, she brushed past the other shooters and lifted their wallets.

"You better give the little lady a rifle what shoots or give her a prize, one o' the two, pal," the wiry man said.

"Well, we'll work somethin' out. We will! Honest!"

What a great actor the counter man was!

"Now, buddy! Now!"

The girl put the wallets in her bag and slipped up beside her man, as if hiding behind him.

"OK," the counter man said, "here's a prize, but now I gotta shut down the gallery for a while."

Just like before, the players complained, the ones who caused the commotion drifted away, and the counter man offered a small refund to everyone. But it didn't blow over like it had before. This time someone besides me was watching from the crowd, someone who didn't see or think like everyone else. This was someone who was too plain and simple-minded to be distracted from what was really going on.

He said, "Hey, wait a minute! That lady just stole all your wallets!"

The men at the counter slapped their back pockets and flew into a rage.

"She did it," the voice said. "That girl right there with that man!"

The voice in the night, the innocent, simple voice of black-and-white justice, belonged to Jack Bastable. The wiry man glared at him and made a move for him.

Jack was in trouble.

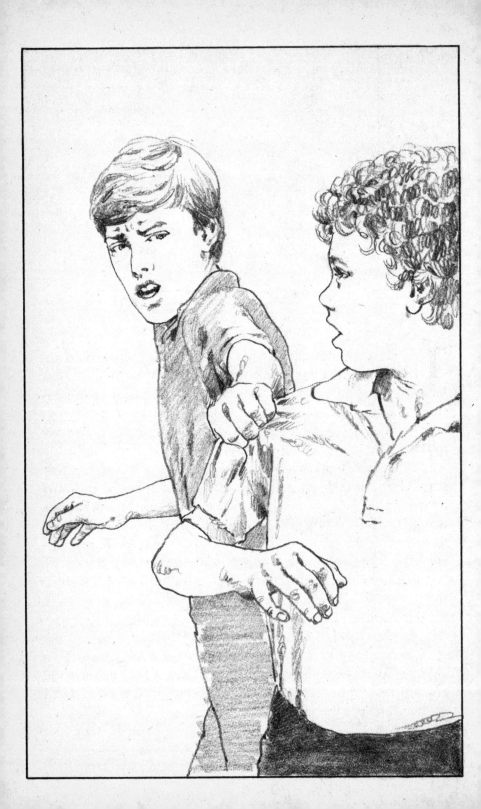

11

Breathless

The girl with the wallets went one way, the counter man another, and the tall, wiry-muscled con artist lit out after Jack. Kyle ducked and scampered between several of the patrons and headed away from the midway, out into a dirt-covered lot that ran along the back of the park in the dark. Jimmy followed him.

I kept an eye on Jack. He looked puzzled and scared. I was scared but not puzzled. Jack had exposed their scam, and now he was going to pay for it. It flashed through my mind that this was all my fault. I was going to have to answer for it, confess it to several of the guys, the Bastables, and worst of all, my parents. But for now I couldn't let anything happen to Jack.

I moved beside him and grasped the elbow of his shirtsleeve. "Do exactly what I say," I whispered.

He turned, surprised. "Dallas!"

"Just do what I say," I repeated.

The tall man was nearly upon us now. In the confusion a big man with coveralls and a straw hat stood between the tall guy and me. "I'm sorry about this," I said to Coveralls, and I pushed him into the tall man.

"Hey!" he bellowed as he fell and almost knocked the other man down.

At the same time I pulled hard on Jack's sleeve and turned him around. "Run, Jack! Run fast! Catch up with Kyle and Jimmy! Go!"

"But, Dallas, that girl stole—"

"Go!"

I slung him into the rest of the crowd, who bounced out of the way and watched him run. He was some runner once he got going. Years of sports had given him a strangely graceful gait that chewed up a lot of ground. I knew he would catch Kyle and Jimmy in a few seconds and that they would be able to lead him over a fence and back to the bike racks, where I hoped everyone else would be waiting.

I stole a glance behind me and saw the tall man coming at me, fire in his eyes. Fortunately, the man in coveralls was just getting back to his feet and the tall man ran into him again. With that, I followed Jack, pumping as furiously as I could, running out into the night, hoping I could outrun an angry man.

I was never more scared in my life. The running robbed me of breath, but so did my fear. I only hoped he was a smoker, short of lung space, and not used to running. I heard the loud clomps of his footsteps in the dust and knew he was wearing heavy boots. He was close, but I didn't think he was gaining on me. I moved to the right and to the left, hoping to lose him, and I sensed him falling farther behind. The problem was, when I looked back I realized he was not alone. Maybe a half dozen others were with him, chasing me.

I saw Jack pass Jimmy and Kyle in the distance and heard Kyle yelling, "Left, Jack, left! Over the fence and right!"

They cleared the fence about twenty seconds ahead of me, and as I scaled it and scooted over I saw that the guys chasing me were still coming. I hoped I had enough breath and strength to get into the crowd at the exit.

I prayed as I ran, pleading for stamina and speed. All I could think of was that this was my fault, my fault, my fault. As terrified as I was, I knew I still had the horror of facing the guys, the Bastables, and my parents. I hoped this was the worst of what I would have to admit, that we escaped.

Something in me wanted to see these bullies get caught too. A lot of people who'd lost watches and wallets would love to see the place cleaned up—even the owners. Who wanted a reputation like that?

I flew past the acres of parked cars and the snakes of cars cruising up to the exit to pick up people leaving the park. I ran past the bike racks where I noticed that all our bikes were still there. Just inside the re-entry gate Jack and Jimmy and Kyle stood panting, bent over, sucking air. Panic was still in their eyes. I showed my hand stamp to the guard.

"Did you tell him?" I asked Jimmy.

"Who knows who you can trust around here?" Jim gasped. "I'm not tellin' anybody. That's your job."

He was right. I had caused the mess; I could try to fix it.

I looked back out across the parking lot. The tall, wiry man and his companions were clambering back over the fence. I only hoped they wouldn't recognize us if they ever saw us again. I would remember his face, as well as his girl friend's. I hoped I would be brave enough to identify him if I ever got the chance.

We called our parents to let them know we would be late, then waited about another half hour to make sure no one was out there waiting to ambush us. We didn't want to be riding our bikes in the darkness and find somebody following us in a car.

The worst part about my night was that I would have to face Mr. Bastable even before I faced my parents. I had to tell him I had failed. I had not done a good job. I had squandered his money and the money I said I was going to split up among the guys who had helped with Jack. I had to apologize and ask his forgiveness and for a chance to prove myself again some day.

Mr. Bastable was pretty good about it. He didn't brush it off, didn't say it was all right. He told me he appreciated my honesty and that he accepted my apology, but that he would have to think about Jack's continued involvement in the Baker Street Sports Club.

"Especially in other activities, like this one. It was too much to ask for you guys to watch Jack."

"No, it wasn't, sir. We should have been able to handle it. This was all my fault."

"Well," he said, "we'll talk about it another time. Good night."

The ride home from there was the longest I'd ever ridden, but it was also too short, if you know what I mean. As long as I live I'll never forget walking into that living room where my dad sat with his paper and my mom with her book, guilt written all over my face.

"How was your day, honey?" my mom asked, as if I would be bubbling with stories of fun and excitement.

I told them the whole story through my tears, and I didn't leave out one detail. It was too late to try to make myself look good. I had failed pitifully, and no amount of sugar coating would change that. Worse than their anger was my parents' surprise and disappointment. I would have done anything not to have hurt them like that, but that's the problem with doing something wrong. You can be forgiven, but nothing changes the fact that you did it. And there are results.

My dad spoke softly but firmly. "You know you'll have to be punished."

I nodded. "I need to be punished, Dad. I feel so bad, I'll accept whatever you say."

"I know you've suffered already," he said. "But your mother and I are going to discuss this and tell you in the morning what we decide. We love you though, Dal. You know that, don't you?"

"That's what makes it all the worse," I said.

I was grounded for a month—even from sports club activities—and I couldn't go to Acres of Fun for the rest of the summer, even with the family. I had to earn money to pay back Mr. Bastable and all the guys. My dad also wanted a report about what I said to the guys in the club. Confessing to them, admitting I had been wrong, and asking their forgiveness was almost as hard as confessing to my parents. Almost.

It changed the way the guys thought about me. I think they had resented my image with their parents of being Mr. Perfect. But they forgave me. And even the ones who had been toughest to get along with—Cory, Kyle, even Nate—were different after that.

Even if they hadn't changed, I know I did.

Moody Press, a ministry of the Moody Bible Institute, is designed for education, evangelization, and edification. If we may assist you in knowing more about Christ and the Christian life, please write us without obligation: Moody Press, c/o MLM, Chicago, Illinois 60610.